D.W. RIDES AGAIN!

Marc Brown

LITTLE, BROWN AND COMPANY

New York ❧ Boston

For Maria Modugno,
who even edits my dedications!

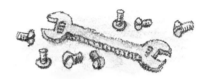

Little, Brown and Company

Hachette Book Group USA
237 Park Avenue, New York, NY 10017
Visit our Web site at www.lb-kids.com

First Edition

D.W.™ is a trademark of Marc Brown.

ISBN 0316113565 (hc)
ISBN 9780316110525 (pb)

Library of Congress Catalog Card Number 93-7192

HC: 10
PB: 10 9

SC

Manufactured in China

"I love my new bike," said D.W.

"Now I can give my tricycle to baby Kate," she said.

"I can go a lot faster on a two-wheeler!"

"Look out!" called Father.

"Are you all right?" asked Father.
"Where are the brakes?" asked D.W.

You have to pedal backward to stop," said Arthur.
Maybe I should give you some lessons. The sooner the better."

"Tomorrow after school is soon enough," said Father.
"Right now it's time for dinner."

The next day after school, D.W. was ready and waiting.

"First thing," said Arthur, "put your helmet on."

"When do we do tricks?" asked D.W. "Teach me some tricks!"

"Pay attention," said Arthur. "This is important."

"Always keep to the right of the road," said Arthur, "and
ride with traffic.

"Watch out for holes and stuff in the road. And remember,"
said Arthur, "Stay alert!

"Now, pull over and I'll teach you the hand signals."

"Use your left hand to signal. This means I'm stopping."

"This means right turn."

"This means left turn."

"What does this mean?" asked D.W.

"It means you'll be back on a tricycle if you don't watch out," said Arthur. "Oh, I almost forgot," he said. "Steer clea of unfriendly dogs!"

"Burn a little rubber!" called D.W. "I don't want to end up a doggy lunch!"

"I could go a lot faster without these yucky training wheels," said D.W. "Look at that little kid. He doesn't have any training wheels."
"Nobody likes a show-off," said Arthur.

"I'm asking Dad to take them off when we get home," said D.W.

But when Father took off the training wheels, D.W. had a very hard time.

"Uh-oh," said Alex.
"I can't watch," said Jenna.

"The training wheels have to go back on," said Father, "but I'll move them up a little higher. You're *almost* ready."

D.W. practiced every day.

She practiced right turns.

Left turns.

he practiced figure-eights

and tiny circles.

All the hard stuff.

After a while, Father thought she was ready.

Mother did, too.

Even Arthur thought she might be ready.

"OK," said Father, "I'll take the training wheels off, and we'll go on a little ride together to see if you're really ready." "Yippee!" said D.W. "I'm really ready. You'll see."

Dad was very nervous.
"Watch this," said D.W.
"Don't show off," said Father. "Watch what you're doing.
Use your brakes!" he called. "Not too fast! Pay attention!"

D.W. came to a perfect stop.
"Dad, are you all right?" she asked.
"Yes," grumbled Father.

"Can I keep my training wheels off?" asked D.W.
"Yes," grumbled Father.
"Yippee!" squealed D.W. "Now *you* can use them."

E BRO
Brown, Marc Tolon.
D.W. rides again! /